Bean Soup Media

www.beansoupmedia.com

The Boy King Who Loves Ice Cream

Written by Toure Muhammad
Illustrated by Hijab Zahraa

For more information, please contact:
Bean Soup Media
773-531-8798
 toure@beansouptimes.com
142 West 62nd Street, Chicago, Illinois, 60621 US

My name is Colin and I have a story to tell,
about a day in life when things didn't go so well.
My stomach hurt and my head pounded too.
I woke up feeling like an old stinky shoe.

You see, my life depends on just one thing,
which makes me want to holler, shout and scream,
chocolate to vanilla and all flavors in between;
I am sad, without some hand-scooped ice cream.

I jumped out of bed and ran to my parent's room,
to alert mom and dad of my possible doom.
"Good morning beloveds! I have something to say.
I need two or three scoops of ice cream today!"

"It's been six days since my last treat.
I know I just woke up, but I feel incomplete.
You know how I get, sickly and bleak,
if I don't get hand-packed ice cream at least once a week."

Dad looked out the window and said, "It is very cold.
To be honest son, the truth must be told.
I scream, you scream, we both scream,
today is a very good day for ice cream!"

I was so happy. I began to sing,
like a young prince who became king;
sitting on my throne eating chocolate chip.
I'd share with my kingdom, "Everyone gets a dip!"

For some reason mom had a big frown.
And this wasn't good, I usually found.
And with a loud ding, guess what hit the ground?
With just one look, mom knocked off my crown.

"Have you done your homework?" she said with a glare.
"Until all of it's done, you'll go nowhere."
I looked at team Dad who looked away.
I was on my own on this cold day.

I went to my room, defeated and beat,
not sure if I'll get my favorite treat.
I wonder how mom would feel,
knowing I died without my favorite meal.

As I grabbed all my pads, workbooks, and more,
I knew my hope was lost as they all hit the floor.
I decided to work as fast as I could.
I'd get my ice cream today. It will be all good.

By noontime, I was just about done
with all of my work, like a good smart son.
It's time to get back on my throne.
I was thinking black cherry on a waffle cone.
I rushed to tell mom, "My work was complete!"
She said "That's great! Now it's time for your treat."

I did a fist pump. I knew she was pleased.
Like dad says "after difficulty comes ease."
But now my dad who was on my team before
said something that made me drop to the floor.
"Son, I know you are excited and I aim to please,
but first clean your room and rake all the leaves."

My heart melted a little. I didn't know what to say.
I'll be sad if I don't get my ice cream today.
First mom sold me out, now it's dad's turn;
I'm lost without ice cream. When will they learn?

I should throw in the towel, ball up, and cry.
No ice cream today, no matter how much I try.
I really don't want to clean my room;
but what choice do I have? "Mom, where's the broom?"

It took some time but my hope was restored.
I said to my parents, "I've done all my chores."
We hopped in the car. My work is done.
Despite all the challenges, looks like I won.
We pulled in front of the Big Ice Cream Shop
to see a huge crowd that made us come to a stop.

As I looked out the window, I saw a strange sight.
People with signs screaming with all their might.
Then a man dressed in all black began to plead,
about police brutality and corporate greed.
He said, "Accept your own and be yourself. Support black
businesses and increase our wealth!"

The owner stormed out and shouted, "What gives?"
The crowd yelled back. "It's time to make
our communities a safe place to live."
The man in all black made everything all clear.
Don't buy from businesses like this one here.
"We're not buying from big box stores today.
Only black-owned places, so send love their way."

My body was frozen as I heard those words.
My stomach hurt more from what I heard.
Mom and Dad, "I've got something to say.
I no longer want ice cream today."

NO JUSTICE NO PEACE

My parents smiled. We grabbed a sign and hit the streets,
with hundreds of people who shouted, "No Justice, No Peace!"
We marched for an hour. I felt so bold.
My feet were not tired and my hands were not cold.

As we turned the corner, I was surprised to see,
another ice cream shop right up the street.
As we got closer, I was in for another shock.
It was cold, but the line was around the block.

A couple was in front, the man with a tray in his hand,
"Free ice cream for all who are taking a stand!
Shawn Michelle's Homemade Ice Cream makes the best,
made with faith and love, I must truly confess."

"Here young man...have a tasty taste.
"Eat it fast! Let none go to waste."
A giant tub in one hand and a scoop in the other.
Yahya dished out ice cream to my father and mother.

His wife Nataki said, "We've got black walnut, strawberry cheesecake, and honey cinnamon graham cracker."
I tried so many. My mouth was so full, I could hardly speak.
My stomach stopped hurting and I was no longer weak.

"Come, young man, try some more soon!
We've got banana pudding, and also blue moon.
Try our pralines-n-cream and peach cobbler too.
Butter pecan and cookies-n-cream all for you."

"What I serve is the best, just like grandma used to make.
So let the world know that there is no debate.
We make this with care, for all the kings and queens.
We roll out the purple carpet when you hit the scene."

"Our tasty treats will make your face grin,
So, take three scoops and fall in love again."

Shawn Michelle's made me feel like a king.
I'm back on my throne with a song to sing,
"I scream, you scream, we all scream
for Shawn Michelle's homemade ice cream!"

Nataki and Yahya Muhammad enjoy ice cream below the portrait of Shawn Michelle, Yahya's late older sister.

The story of Colin and his love of ice cream is fictional, but Shawn Michelle's Homemade Ice Cream is not only a real ice cream shop, but the home of really delicious ice cream. Shawn Michelle's is a family-owned ice cream parlor that uses real ingredients to make real ice cream. They are bridging the gap of old fashioned homemade goodness and creating new memories of homemade desserts. So, go back down memory lane, but this time, bring your children too!

You must try one of Shawn Michelle's signature homemade ice cream flavors like vanilla, butter pecan or black walnut. They make all of their ice cream with the best ingredients to generate the best results. Try it for yourself!

Visit Shawn Michelle's at www.shawnmichelles.com or in Chicago at 46 E. 47th Street in historic Bronzeville.

TOURE MUHAMMAD is the creator of Bean Soup Media, LLC, a digital media and marketing company that helps restaurants and realtors grow their brand. Today, Bean Soup Media, LLC publishes Bean Soup Times and Black Chicago Eats, which both promote Black-owned businesses.

Other books written by Toure Muhammad include:

Both can be found at www.beansoupmedia.com

www.ingramcontent.com/pod-product-compliance
Lightning Source LLC
Chambersburg PA
CBHW041012170626
46815CB00003B/275